Disney
5-Minute Easter Stories
Disney PRESS
Los Angeles • New York

Logo Applies to Text Stock Only

For information address Disney Press, 1200 Grand Central Avenue, Glendale, California 91201.

Printed in the United States of America

First Hardcover Edition, January 2020

Library of Congress Control Number: 2018967842

1 3 5 7 9 10 8 6 4 2

ISBN 978-1-368-04194-2

FAC-038091-19326

For more Disney Press fun, visit www.disneybooks.com

Contents

Thumper and the Egg

Thumper woke up bright and early, ready to explore! It had stormed the day before, and he wanted to see what the wind and rain had blown out into the open.

As he hopped around exploring, he saw a mouse scurrying toward its tree, picked a pretty pink flower that had bloomed, and sniffed at a ladybug that had landed on a leaf.

Then he saw a blue feather. He hopped toward it to catch it!

Thumper followed the feather over a hill and down to the river, but he stopped abruptly when he came across something small and blue. Curiously, he bent down and sniffed it. *Sniff, sniff.*

Quiet giggles pulled Thumper's attention away from the object.

He looked up and saw his four younger sisters—Trixie, Tessie, Daisy, and Ria—watching him from a log. They had followed him to the river and waited as he examined the strange object.

"Come over here and look at what I found!" Thumper called.

The four bunny sisters hopped to meet their brother.

"Whatcha doin', Thumper?" Trixie asked. She had a big bushy tail and always wanted to know what was going on.

"Treasure huntin'," he explained.

The bunnies looked at the smooth round object.

“It’s pretty. What is it?” Tessie asked. She was the youngest bunny.

“It’s a robin’s egg, silly,” Thumper said.

Daisy cheered. "Oh, a birdie!" She was excited. She loved making new friends.

"But what's it doing here?" Trixie asked. "I thought robins kept their eggs in nests up in trees."

"You're right!" Thumper said. "It must have gotten knocked down in the storm last night. What should we do?"

The bunnies began to worry about the egg. They thought the mama robin was probably worried, too.

Ria hopped over to Thumper. "You need to keep it warm and happy until it hatches," she said. Ria was a smart bunny, so the group knew she was right.

"Good idea, Ria! We've gotta make the egg feel like it's wrapped up in a soft, cozy blanket!" Thumper told his sisters.

Ria, Trixie, and Tessie hopped to it, gathering leaves from nearby bushes.

Trixie started piling leaves on top of the egg one by one.

"That'll take forever!" Tessie said. "We should put a bunch of leaves on top all at once! The egg will be warmer faster."

"No, no, no! We have to surround the egg, not cover it. Like this," Ria corrected them both.

While his sisters argued, Thumper tried to figure out what to do next. Whenever he was confused, he usually asked his mama for help.

“That’s it!” Thumper said to his sisters. “Where is the mama robin? She’ll know the right thing to do.”

“Let’s go find her!” Tessie said, excited for their next adventure.

“We can’t all go, or someone else may try to take the egg,” Daisy said. “Thumper and I will stay here and make sure the egg stays happy.”

So Trixie, Ria, and Tessie hopped off to find the egg’s mama.

Thumper thumped his foot while his sisters were away. He was nervous.

"How will we keep it happy?" Thumper asked Daisy.

"Well, I'm happy when I sing. Let's sing to it!" Daisy decided.

"Um, I don't know if it can hear us in there—" Thumper began to say. But before he finished, Daisy started singing at the top of her lungs.

Birds, moles, and turtles all gathered around to hear her sing, but Thumper couldn't tell if the egg was happy.

After a while, Daisy ran out of songs.

"Well, what now?" Thumper asked.

"Let's dance!" Daisy exclaimed.

"I don't think it can see us—" But again, Thumper didn't get to finish his sentence. This time it was because Daisy grabbed his paw and made him dance, too!

Some ducklings and even a turtle joined in on the fun, but Thumper *still* couldn't tell if the egg was happy!

After they were all done dancing, Thumper thought that maybe the egg would like one of his tricks instead.

He picked up his blue feather, snuck up on Daisy while she was watching the egg, and tickled her!

Daisy began rolling on the ground with laughter.

Daisy's laughter was so loud that the bunnies didn't hear their father hop up.

"Thumper, now what did I tell you about tickling your sisters?" Papa Bunny said.

"But it was to keep the egg happy," Thumper said. "We tried making it comfy, and singing and dancing, but nothing seemed to work. So I thought maybe if Daisy laughed, the egg would laugh, too!"

Just then, Thumper and Papa Bunny heard shouting and the sound of three little bunnies hopping toward them. They turned to see Trixie, Tessie, and Ria appear with a nest of twigs. A mama robin flew above them.

After his sisters set the nest down, Thumper placed the egg inside. Then the mama robin flew into the nest and covered the egg with her wing.

Soon the bunnies heard a crackling noise. They all gathered around as a baby bird popped out of the shell!

The bunnies all cheered. They had taken good care of the egg!

Thumper gave Daisy the pink flower and blue feather he'd found earlier. "Thanks for helping me keep the egg happy."

"It was fun," she said. "Plus, I learned a new trick." Then she began to tickle her brother!

The Wishing Well

One bright spring morning, before she met the Dwarfs or the Prince, Snow White leaned over her balcony to catch a glimpse of the flowery meadow. But this was no ordinary spring.

It hadn't rained much, and there weren't nearly as many flowers as usual.

Snow White tried to listen for the far-off tinkling of the forest stream, but instead, she heard a cry that sounded as if it was coming from the wishing well below her balcony!

She raced down the castle stairs and over to the wishing well.

Snow White peered into the well, and she was surprised to find a bunny inside. It was sipping from a puddle of water. "You must be very thirsty," she said.

Startled, the bunny tried to climb out, but it was too small.

“It’s much easier to get in than to get out!” called Snow White. “Don’t worry. I’ll help you.” She cupped her hands and leaned over so the bunny could hop into them, but it couldn’t jump high enough.

Almost . . . but not quite.

“I know,” Snow White said, “I can bring you up in the bucket.” She lowered the bucket slowly, but when she tried to raise it again with the bunny inside, the rope broke!

Snow White closed her eyes and wished for the bunny to be safely out of the well.

When she opened them again, a squirrel had joined the bunny, leaning down to drink out of the puddle. *Perhaps there isn't enough water in the well to make a proper wish*, Snow White thought.

Eager to save the animals, Snow White decided to ask her stepmother for help.

But when she reached the Queen's chambers, she saw her stepmother staring into her magic mirror, enchanted by what she saw there. Snow White tiptoed away. She knew not to disturb the Queen when she was talking to her mirror.

Snow White slowly descended the castle stairs, thinking about the animals in the well. As she looked down at her feet, she thought about how each stone step formed the grand staircase.

It gave her an idea!

With renewed hope, Snow White headed for the trees. She sped through the meadow and into the brush until she came to a trail of stones deep in the forest.

Snow White bent down to lift one of the heavy rocks, then hauled it out of the woods.

Snow White rested the stone on the edge of the wishing well and peeked inside to check on the animals.

She saw that a raccoon, a chipmunk, and a skunk had joined the others trapped inside.

"Watch out!" Snow White called before carefully dropping the stone down along the inner edge of the well.

Without uttering another word, she dashed off into the forest once more.

Soon Snow White returned with another stone, and she dropped it into the well the same way as the first. "Push this one next to the first rock," she told the animals. Then she brought another stone, and another.

As news spread of Snow White's efforts, animals from throughout the forest came to help.

When they were all done, Snow White and the animals admired their work. "It's not as fancy as the one in the castle, but it will have to do," said Snow White. With the help of the animals, Snow White had built a staircase!

The bunny hopped up the stairs first, followed by the squirrel, the raccoon, and the chipmunk. Everyone kept a safe distance from the skunk!

When all the animals were out, a soft spring rain began to fall. Snow White celebrated by singing a happy song.

From that day forward, Snow White and the forest animals became close friends. After the rain finally arrived, flowers bloomed everywhere, and the bushes were bursting with berries. And there was plenty of water in the well for making wishes.

The Case of the Disappearing Easter Eggs

Detective Judy Hopps and her partner from the Zootopia Police Department, Nick Wilde, were in Judy's hometown to celebrate Easter with her family.

Officer Clawhauser, having never been to Bunnyburrow before, went along as well.

Together, the three friends hid chocolate Easter eggs for all the children of Bunnyburrow to find.

After they'd laid out dozens of the eggs in an open field, Nick gathered the empty candy bags and went to put them in the trash can. He turned around to admire their work, and his mouth fell open.

"Hey, Hopps. We have a problem."

“What’s wrong?” Judy asked, looking back at the field.

Her eyes widened. All the candy eggs they had placed there were gone!

"I say we split up and check the perimeter of the field for evidence," Judy said. "Call out if you find anything. We are going to find those missing eggs!"

Slowly, the three detectives circled the field.

Nick slid his watchful eyes left and right.

Clawhauser used his excellent balance to explore the playground.

Judy kept her nose close to the ground and her ears up for odd noises. She heard something in the distance, over the hill.

She was about to investigate when Nick called out to her and Clawhauser. "You guys! I got something over here!"

It was a trail of bear prints.

"Good work!" Judy said. "Why don't you guys follow them? I heard something over the hill I want to check out."

So Clawhauser and Nick followed the trail into the woods. Soon they found themselves at the door of a cozy cottage.

Nick stepped forward and knocked on the door. "ZPD! We'd like to ask you a few questions."

A family of bears answered the door. “Can I help you?” the father bear asked.

“You took our chocolate, didn’t you?” Clawhauser accused, spotting a brown smudge on the boy bear’s sweater.

The father bear looked at Clawhauser, astonished. “This is just brown paint. We were painting this morning.”

Nick took a whiff for good measure. He could tell the stain wasn’t chocolate.

“Plus, we wouldn’t have done that,” the little girl bear said. “Me and my brother are allergic to chocolate.”

“Thank you,” Nick told them. “You’ve been very helpful.”

Meanwhile, Judy arrived at the top of the hill and found a brand-new basketball court on the other side. Several giraffes in green and blue were finishing up a game and preparing to leave.

Judy introduced herself, showing one of the giraffes her ZPD badge. She was hoping the giraffe could answer a few questions about the investigation.

"Did you happen to notice chocolate eggs at the field over there?" Judy asked.

"Oh, yes," the giraffe said.

"Did you happen to see the chocolate . . . disappear?" Judy continued.

"I did, actually," the giraffe answered. "All of the eggs just suddenly sank into the ground."

Judy was confused. "How could that be?"

"I'm not sure, but I can see from here that none of the eggs you hid in the trees disappeared," the giraffe replied, directing Judy's attention back to the field.

Judy stood on her toes to look. Sure enough, she could see some eggs on low tree branches.

"So it was only the field that was affected," Judy said, turning this over in her mind. "I should go check in with my partners. Thanks so much for your help!"

Judy found Nick and Clawhauser in the middle of the field. They updated each other on what they'd found out. And then, suddenly, there was a faint knocking noise.

"Wait a minute!" Judy said. "Did you hear that?"

A spray of dirt flew up from the ground nearby.

"There's a hole!" Clawhauser cried.

"Stop right there!" Nick called out.

The creature froze.

"Come out of the hole," Judy said.

Once the critter emerged, the officers could tell he was a prairie dog.

Nick began the interrogation. "Sir, do you happen to know what became of the approximately one thousand chocolate eggs it took us over an hour to hide in this field?"

The prairie dog sighed. “I’m afraid my kids took them.”

“Your kids?” Judy and Nick said in unison.

“Well, yes. And my nieces and nephews,” the prairie dog replied. As if on cue, the ground rumbled and a pack of young prairie dogs appeared. “The town built a basketball court right over our heads! It was so noisy, so we moved to this field last week. Because of all the hubbub, we haven’t had a chance to shop for Easter candy,” the older prairie dog explained. “This morning, the kids woke up and smelled chocolate. . . . I’m afraid they couldn’t resist.”

"Well, thank you for being honest with us," Judy said. "But listen, kids. You can't steal from other animals."

"I'm afraid we have to hand down some sort of punishment," Nick said, hiding a smile.

“I think community service is appropriate,” Judy said. “Community service is helping out in your neighborhood to make life better for the animals around you. Today I think we’ll start with you kids helping us hide more eggs in the field.”

"Hey, Carrots," Nick whispered to Judy a little while later. "I bought one extra bag for you, me, and Clawhauser to split."

Judy looked around. "Where *is* Clawhauser?"

They found him in the truck . . . shoveling the last of the eggs into his mouth.

"That chocolate was for all of us!" Nick cried.

"Sorry." Clawhauser stopped chewing. "I guess I gotta do community service?"

Mater and the Easter Buggy

Easter was just one day away, and the cars in Radiator Springs were revving up for some fun. As Lightning McQueen drove down Main Street, he saw his friends getting ready for the holiday.

Red, the fire truck, was planting taillight tulip bulbs. Flo, the 1950s show car, was showing off her fancy new Easter colors. Lizzie, the Model T, was having a spring sale. Fillmore, the van, was decorating oilcans for the town's annual Easter can hunt.

But no one was more excited about Easter than Mater, the tow truck. “I can’t wait for the Easter Buggy!” he told Lightning.

Lightning just smiled. He didn’t believe in the Easter Buggy.

“I’m going to stay up all night,” Mater said.

“No one’s ever seen the Easter Buggy,” Lightning reminded him.

“I know it,” Mater said. “That’s why I have a plan.”

Lightning realized his friend was serious. “But what if the Easter Buggy doesn’t show up?” he asked.

“Of course he’ll come,” Mater said with a laugh. “It’s Easter, ain’t it? Now, ’scuse me, buddy. I gotta finish gettin’ ready. This is gonna be the best Easter ever!”

Lightning knew he had to do something. If the Easter Buggy didn't show, Mater would be so disappointed!

So Lightning picked up some Easter cans from Fillmore's, springs from Lizzie's curio shop, and a dozen lug nuts and a quart of coolant from Flo's.

Last of all, Lightning picked up some headlamps for an Easter Buggy disguise and headed back to Mater's tow yard. "Now I'll just wait until Mater falls asleep," he said. He hid by a nearby fence, and then he waited . . . and waited.

At last, Mater's eyes closed. Lightning's plan was to fill his friend's Easter tire so when Mater woke up, he'd think the Easter Buggy had come!

But Lightning accidentally rolled over an alarm Mater had set up.

"He's here!" cried Mater, waking up.

"Lightning!" Mater said. "Did ya see him?"

"See who?" asked Lightning.

"The Easter Buggy!" Mater exclaimed.

Mater checked his Easter tire. "Nothing yet," he said. "But he set off the alarm. He must be around here somewhere."

Lightning had to think fast. "I'll bet he's stopping by Luigi's. Why don't you catch him over there?"

"Good thinking, buddy," Mater replied as he sped off toward Luigi's tire shop.

Lightning followed quietly behind. "Good ole Mater." He chuckled to himself. "I should have known he'd set a booby trap for the Easter Buggy."

Mater pulled up in front of Luigi's Casa Della Tires and set down his Easter tire. Lightning hid and waited for Mater to fall asleep again.

Soon he heard Mater's snores. Lightning tried to sneak over to fill Mater's Easter tire. But he bumped into a stack of tires. . . .

CRASH! The tower of tires tumbled down around Lightning and Mater.

"The Easter Buggy's here!" Mater shouted. Then, to Lightning, he said, "Dadgum! We missed him again. Where do you think he'll go next?"

"Er, what about Ramone's?" Lightning suggested.

"That's it!" cried Mater. "We're hot on his trail now."

Together they drove to Ramone's House of Body Art. "We'll keep watch together this time," Mater said.

But as soon as he got inside Ramone's garage, Mater fell asleep.

"Now's my chance," Lightning said to himself. He snuck toward Mater's Easter tire. "No Easter Buggy traps. No tower of tires. Looks like the path is—"

Lightning's back end accidentally hit the shelves filled with paint. He was covered in bright Easter colors!

"Look at that," Mater said. "The Easter Buggy gave you a new paint job!"

"Heyyy, I think I know where to find the Easter Buggy now," Mater told Lightning as they left Ramone's.

"You do?" Lightning asked.

"Yup, the sun's almost up. He must be on his way out of town!" said Mater.

So Lightning and Mater drove to the end of the paved road. "We won't miss him this time," Mater said.

As soon as Mater falls asleep again, I'll fill his Easter tire, Lightning thought.

But by then Lightning was very tired. Before long, he fell asleep . . .

RADIATOR
SPRINGS

Leaving
So Soon?

. . . and slept until morning.

"Wake up, Lightning!" Mater shouted. "The Easter Buggy was here!"

"Oh, no!" Lightning hadn't had a chance to fill Mater's Easter tire!

But to Lightning's amazement, Mater's tire was full of treats.

"Look," Mater said. "He gave you a bunch of goodies. He's the best!"

That wasn't all. The Easter Buggy had left something for every car in Radiator Springs.

"That's a beautiful sight, man," said Fillmore.

"What a great Easter!" Flo agreed.

“I still can’t figure out who filled everybody’s Easter tires,” Lightning said.

“It was the Easter Buggy,” Mater replied. “That’s what I keep tellin’ you.”

“Well, Mater,” said Lightning, “maybe you’re right.”

“*Maybe?* I know I’m right!” Mater said.

“Happy Easter, Mater,” said Lightning.

“Happy Easter, buddy!” said Mater.

The Easter Egg Hunt

It was a beautiful spring day in the Hundred-Acre Wood. As Pooh was heading to Rabbit's house for an Easter egg hunt, he felt a rumbling in his tummy.

Pooh had a worrisome thought—what if Rabbit was out of honey? He decided to grab a jar from his cabinet. He didn't want to show up to the Easter egg hunt empty-handed.

But when Pooh arrived, he was, in fact, empty-handed. He had stopped along the way and eaten every last drop of honey.

Soon Pooh spotted his friends. He wondered why it seemed as if they had been waiting for a while. He had left exactly on time.

"Happy Easter!" Pooh called to them.

Pooh's friends were excited to see him. "Happy Easter, Pooh!"

Rabbit hopped onto a tree stump. "Everyone, I have hidden Easter eggs all over the woods. Whoever finds the most will win a special feast. Get ready, get set . . . go!"

"Today is going to be an *egg*-cellent day!" Tigger seemed very excited. "Tiggers love contests."

Pooh, Piglet, Roo, Kanga, and Eeyore walked into the woods. Tigger bounced off in another direction. "Good luck, everyone!" he shouted.

Pooh knew that Rabbit was a good Easter egg hider. He wanted to be an even better Easter egg finder.

"Hmm . . ." Pooh said. "If I were Rabbit, I would hide an Easter egg in . . ." Pooh trailed off when he spotted some yellow flowers. "Daffodils!" He felt the ground under the leaves.

"A yellow egg!" Pooh put it into his straw basket. But Pooh didn't know his Easter basket had a hole in the bottom. The yellow egg had fallen out onto the grass.

Piglet was not far behind Pooh. Soon he found the yellow egg. "Oh my, lucky me!" Piglet carefully tucked the egg into his own Easter basket.

Meanwhile, Pooh was looking behind a rock. "A purple egg!" Pooh placed it in the basket and began to daydream about all the delicious honey he would eat if he won.

He didn't notice when this egg, too, slipped out of his basket.

Not far behind, Roo hopped by the same rock. He hadn't found a single egg yet. Roo stopped hopping and looked down at the grass. There was Pooh's egg! "Oh, goody! Purple is my favorite color!"

Meanwhile, Pooh found a green egg in a tall clump of grass. "This may very well be the luckiest Easter ever!" But this egg also fell out of his basket.

A little while later, Tigger was bouncing along when he saw a large green egg. But he had no idea it had fallen out of Pooh's Easter basket. Tigger stopped bouncing long enough to pick it up. "Hoo-hoo-hoo-hoo! I'm on my way to winning!"

Pooh carefully looked through a bed of pink wildflowers. There, he spotted a red egg on the ground. "I think it is nearly time for a snack," Pooh said, rubbing his rumbly tummy thoughtfully.

Before long, Eeyore rambled by the pink flowers. He had not especially wanted to look for Easter eggs. Then he spotted Pooh's red egg and supposed it would be rather nice to win Rabbit's contest.

Nearby in a meadow, Pooh realized it was almost time to return. He tucked one last egg into his Easter basket and walked up a hill toward Rabbit's house. Unknown to Pooh, this egg fell out and rolled away, too!

Kanga was also on her way back to Rabbit's house. She had not found any eggs, but she did not mind. She thought the hunt had been great fun. Just then, she saw the blue egg next to a log and picked it up.

Soon everyone was back at Rabbit's house. Rabbit once again stood on top of a tree stump. "Time is up!" he announced.

Piglet showed his friends the yellow egg he had found. Roo took out a purple egg.

Tigger held a large green one. “I pounced, bounced, and triple-trounced until I wrestled this egg to the ground!”

Eeyore displayed his red egg. Then Kanga showed her pretty blue egg.

Finally, it was Pooh's turn. He looked inside his straw basket—and it was empty! Pooh wondered where all his Easter eggs had gone. "Oh, bother! Perhaps the eggs decided to hide again."

Piglet looked at the basket in Pooh's hands and poked his hand through the opening. "Oh, look, Pooh Bear. There's a hole in this basket.

"Pooh, you may have my yellow egg. It might have been yours before it was mine." Piglet held out the egg.

Roo hopped forward. "You can have mine, too."

“Here, buddy bear. Tiggers like to win fair and square.” Tigger added his green egg to the ones in Pooh’s arms.

Eeyore thought finding such a pretty egg had probably been too good to be true, so he gave it to Pooh.

Then Kanga took her bright blue egg to Pooh and gently placed it on the very top of the pile.

Rabbit walked over to Pooh. Suddenly, the red egg began to wobble. Rabbit caught it as it fell and put it on the ground. Then he counted up all the eggs. "One, two, three, four, five. Pooh is the winner!"

Then Pooh realized something. His friends had shared their eggs with him. If he had won an Easter feast, he wanted to share it with them! He was feeling very hungry, though. "Is there enough for everyone?" he asked Rabbit.

Rabbit grinned. “Of course. I thought we should all celebrate Easter together.”

“Is there enough honey?” Pooh wondered.

“I always keep lots of honey on hand. You never know when a pooh bear will show up,” Rabbit said, smiling.

Pooh and his friends had a great feast.

"This was the most *egg*-cellent Easter ever, *egg*-specially the egg hunt!" Tigger cheered.

Pooh agreed, but he was too sticky to do anything except nod. It had been a wonderful Easter, indeed.

The Surprise Ballet

One beautiful spring morning, Cinderella and Prudence, the castle's governess, strolled through the gardens. Part of Prudence's job was to help Cinderella with her duties as princess, and an important event was coming up.

"Next week, the northern nobles arrive for their annual spring visit," Prudence said. "It is your job to host their afternoon tea reception."

Prudence led Cinderella to a dark, stuffy room. “This is where the event has always been held,” she said.

“But why sit inside if you’re visiting in the spring?” asked Cinderella.

“It is tradition,” Prudence said, “just as it is tradition for there to be entertainment at the reception. A ballet troupe will perform their spring dance.”

“Ballet?” Cinderella exclaimed. “How wonderful! I used to take ballet lessons!

“I loved learning to leap and spin and kick and balance on my toes!” said Cinderella. “I used to perform for my parents in our garden.”

“But now you are a princess,” Prudence said. “You are expected to *host* the entertainment, not *be* the entertainment.”

But Cinderella had an idea. She told Prudence that she would take care of the performance. She was going to plan a surprise!

The next day, the ballet troupe arrived to begin rehearsing. Cinderella asked if there was room for one more person in their show. She wanted to start a *new* tradition.

First they needed to find Cinderella a costume. All the dancers would be dressed as animals for their spring performance.

Cinderella tried a brown deer costume, a gray rabbit costume, and a bright red bird costume. They were all lovely, but none felt quite right.

Meanwhile, Prudence was getting curious. What surprise was Cinderella planning?

"Maybe I'll just go in and see if they need anything," she said.

When Prudence opened the door, the dancers quickly held out costumes to cover Cinderella.

"Hello, Prudence," said Cinderella. "You weren't trying to ruin the surprise, were you?"

"O-oh," stammered Prudence, "of course not, Princess."

The next morning, Cinderella showed the troupe the palace gardens. They picked a few flowers from each bed and began to weave them into long garlands to use as decorations for the performance.

Prudence was getting more and more anxious.
She needed to know what Cinderella was planning!

Then it was time to rehearse. Cinderella hadn't done ballet in a while. The first time she tried to stand on the tips of her toes, she stumbled and almost fell. She tried to do a graceful spin, but it made her dizzy. Then Cinderella tried to do a high kick, but she knocked down some of the set.

She could have gotten upset, but instead she laughed. She knew she just needed to practice with the other dancers.

The day before the performance, the rehearsal went much better. At the end, the other dancers clapped for her. She had come a long way!

Outside, Prudence heard the applause. Her curiosity rose again. She had to see what Cinderella was up to! She peered through the window.

Cinderella spotted her. She knew Prudence wouldn't give up.

"Prudence, would you like to help with the surprise?" Cinderella asked.

Prudence was relieved. "Yes, please!"

The afternoon of the reception, the doors opened. The northern nobles, along with the Prince, the King, and the Grand Duke, filed into the room, where Prudence was waiting for them.

She swept the velvet draperies aside. Sunlight poured into the room through the open glass doors. Outside was a stage covered in flowers!

Everyone stepped into the fresh air. They smelled the gorgeous flowers and heard birds singing sweetly. Smiling, they took their seats for the performance.

"Where is the princess?" the Grand Duke murmured to Prudence.

Prudence patted his arm. "Wait and see," she said. "It's a surprise."

A moment later, the dance began! The troupe leaped and spun onto the stage. Dancing in front of the others was the featured ballerina, costumed as a beautiful swan.

The dancers began to lift and toss each other into the air. With their strong muscles, they seemed to fly across the stage and land light as feathers.

At the end of the performance, the swan ballerina performed a beautiful solo. She rose onto the tips of her toes, kicking and spinning with perfect balance.

Everyone clapped as the troupe lined up to take their bows. Then the dancers swept off their masks, and the audience gasped. The swan ballerina was Cinderella!

Soon the whole audience was on their feet, cheering for the troupe and their performing princess.

Prudence smiled. “Perhaps this is the start of a new spring tradition.”

Cinderella laughed. “I couldn’t agree more!”

Who's Afraid of the Easter Bunny?

"Oh, boy!" Bonnie cheered. "It's almost Easter! There's chocolate and jelly beans and a big Easter egg hunt! And the Easter Bunny, of course!"

Bonnie looked at Woody's cowboy hat. "Oh, no. That won't do at all," she said. "You can't be a cowboy at Easter. You have to be a bunny!"

Bonnie grabbed a pipe cleaner and twisted it around until it looked like a pair of rabbit ears. Then she placed it on Woody's head.

“Nice ears,” Hamm joked when she had left the room.

“Okay, okay,” Woody said, putting his hat back on. “Hey, Rex . . .” Woody turned to talk to the dinosaur. “Rex?”

“I’m down here,” someone called from under the bed.

Buzz and Woody climbed down to see Rex.

“What are you doing?” Buzz asked.

“Didn’t you hear Bonnie?” Rex said. “The Easter Bunny is coming! We have to hide!”

“I know I’m going to regret asking this,” Hamm said. “What’s wrong with the Easter Bunny?”

“What’s *wrong* with the Easter Bunny?” Rex shouted. “It’s a talking bunny!”

"We lived with Andy for years," Woody said. "And every year he got tons of candy, but we never saw an actual bunny deliver it."

Rex shook his head. "Just because we didn't *see* the Easter Bunny doesn't mean it wasn't there! How can you be so sure?"

"Well, I . . . ummm . . ." Woody began. But he couldn't answer Rex's question. The truth was he *couldn't* be sure.

"Actually," Mr. Pricklepants said, stepping forward, "the legend of the Easter Bunny is quite old. Any story that has managed to survive so long most likely is true."

"See?" Rex shouted. "I told you! It's coming to get us!"

"I don't know," said Trixie. "Wouldn't it be cool to see the actual Easter Bunny?"

"*Maybe* you're right," Rex said.

"That's the spirit!" said Buzz. "I'm sure it's nothing. I mean, really, a talking rabbit? That's just silly."

Rex still wasn't sure who to believe. Buzz and Woody were usually right, but what if this time they were wrong?

Either way, Rex knew he couldn't hide forever. He had begun to climb back to his spot on the shelf when something caught his eye. "What's that?" he said in a panic. "Did the Easter Bunny leave it there?"

"It's just some plastic grass," Jessie said. "Bonnie's mom probably bought it at the store for Easter."

Easter drew closer until, finally, the dreaded day had arrived. Rex didn't want to face the Easter Bunny alone, but he had a problem. Bonnie had left him in the kitchen.

Rex hopped down from the table and saw something suspicious. Willing himself to be brave, Rex took a step closer. It was a chocolate bunny!

Had the Easter Bunny left it?

Rex did his best to stay calm, but he kept finding more signs of the Easter Bunny!

As Rex made his way back to Bonnie's room, he spotted a line of jelly beans on the floor.

Rex followed the jelly bean trail down the hall and into the living room. His eyes landed on something under the table. It was a piece of fluffy white fur!

Rex thought for sure the fur belonged to the Easter Bunny! With a terrified scream, Rex dove under the couch. He had been brave. Now it was time to hide!

Just then, Rex heard a noise. Someone—or something—was coming.

Rex peered out at the living room and saw a big, fluffy white foot come into view.

Rex scooted farther under the couch. Squeezing his eyes shut, he waited for whatever it was to leave.

“Bonnie, what did I tell you about eating in the living room? If you can’t pick up the jelly beans you drop, you can’t eat them in here.”

Rex opened his eyes. He knew that voice! It wasn’t the Easter Bunny. It was Bonnie’s mom, and she was dressed in a white bunny suit. The piece of rabbit fur must have come from her costume!

“Let’s go!” her mom shouted. “Our guests will be here any minute, and I’d like you to be here to greet them with me.”

“It’s party time, it’s party time!” Bonnie sang as she ran into the living room.

Rex knew this was his moment to sneak back to Bonnie’s room.

“I did it!” Rex shouted as he burst through the bedroom door. “I found the Easter Bunny!”

“You did?” Woody asked. “It’s real?”

Rex shook his head. “It’s Bonnie’s mom. She’s wearing a bunny suit for an Easter party. I followed clues and tracked her down.”

“Wow!” Buzz said. “That was very brave.”

Rex nodded. “You were right,” he said. “I was worried about nothing!”

Woody pulled his bunny ears off a shelf and placed them on Rex's head. "I think you earned these."

Rex adjusted the ears and looked at himself in the mirror. "Hey, not bad," he said.

Just then, Bonnie and her friends raced into her bedroom. "Come on," she shouted, scooping up her toys. "It's time for the Easter egg hunt!"

Outside, Bonnie dumped her toys in the side yard. "You wait right here," Bonnie told them as she ran off. "I'll be back after the Easter egg hunt!"

As Bonnie and her friends searched for eggs in the backyard, the toys decided to have some fun of their own with a game of hide-and-seek.

"Ready or not, here I come!" Jessie shouted.

One by one, Jessie tracked down the other toys. Soon only Mr. Pricklepants was still missing.

Just when the toys had started to worry, Mr. Pricklepants came through a hedge. "Ah, there you are," he said. "If you will come with me, I do believe there is something you need to see."

Curious, the toys followed Mr. Pricklepants back into the bushes.

"Quiet now," the hedgehog warned. "You wouldn't want to scare it away."

"Scare what away?" Rex asked. The dinosaur pushed aside the leaves . . .

. . . and promptly passed out.

"You see?" Mr. Pricklepants said, pointing to a big brown bunny in an Easter basket. "The legend of the Easter Bunny is true!"

The Spring Parade

It was a beautiful spring day. The breeze was soft, the sun was warm, and birds were singing happily. Elsa and Anna were picking wildflowers in a field not far from town.

"I can't believe it's finally spring," Anna said, looking around the lush green meadow.

Elsa grinned. "I love spring," she said. "Remember when we were kids and I used to lead—"

"The spring parade!" Anna interrupted. The spring parade was one of her happiest childhood memories. "I *loved* that parade. We haven't had a spring parade since we were little kids."

Elsa nodded. "Now that the gates are open, we should have it again. Starting this year!"

Anna clapped her hands. "You'll look so great at the head of the parade," she told her sister.

Elsa grinned slyly. "Not me. *You!*"

Anna, Elsa, and their friends started planning the parade the very next day.

"Marching band?" Elsa asked.

"Already rehearsing," Kristoff said.

"Flowers?" Anna asked.

"I've been collecting them all—*achooo*—week!" Olaf said, sniffling.

Next on the parade planning checklist was clothing, so Anna and Elsa went to search the royal wardrobe.

"How about this?" Anna asked, putting a silly hat on Elsa.

Elsa giggled and held up some boots. "These are definitely you," she told Anna.

Soon the sisters were laughing so hard at the goofy clothes that they could barely stand.

"Okay, it's time to get serious," Elsa said. "You need something special to wear to the parade!"

With a little help from Anna's friends, the parade was shaping up beautifully. It was going to be exactly like it had been when Anna and Elsa were kids!

The last thing on the planning list was for Anna to find a horse to ride in the parade.

Anna and Olaf headed to the royal stables to find the right horse. Anna thought the first horse seemed promising . . . until he tried to eat Olaf's nose!

"Hey!" Olaf giggled. "That tickles!"

Next Anna saw an elegant horse by the pond.

"This is Lady Crystalbrook Shinytoes the Fourth," the head groom said.

Lady Crystalbrook Shinytoes the Fourth stepped toward Anna . . . and tripped over her own feet. She fell right into the pond!

"Oh, dear," Anna said.

“How about him?” Olaf asked, pointing at a big, strong horse.

“This is Dauntless,” the groom said.

As Anna stepped forward to pet the horse, a leaf fluttered by in the wind. When Dauntless saw the leaf, his eyes widened. With a loud, frightened whinny, he turned and ran away as fast as he could.

“I do *not* think you should ride *him*,” Olaf said.

Hours later, Anna was at her wit's end. They had met every horse, but they hadn't found the right one. "I don't know what to do," she said. "Maybe we should just cancel the parade."

“Cancel the parade?”

Anna and Olaf looked up to find Kristoff and Sven entering the stable. “Why would you do that?” Kristoff asked.

“I can’t find the right horse to lead the parade,” Anna said.

“Hmmm, I think I know just the fellow for the job. But he isn’t exactly a horse,” Kristoff said, slinging his arm around Sven’s shoulders.

“Sven is *perfect*!” Anna exclaimed. “He’s loyal, and brave, and smart!”

“And handsome,” Kristoff added.

“And handsome,” Anna agreed.

Anna introduced Sven to the royal stables' grooms. "He's going to be leading the parade with me," she explained. "So he needs to look extra fancy."

The grooms set to work on Sven. They oiled his hooves. They polished his antlers. And they brushed and brushed and brushed his fur.

When the royal grooms were done with Sven, he positively shone!

"Sven," Anna said, "you look Svendid!" She elbowed Elsa. "Get it? *Sven*did?"

"I get it," Elsa said with a smile. "But I think there's something missing."

Elsa hung a huge flower wreath around Sven's neck.

"There," she said. "Now you're perfect."

Olaf jumped up and down with excitement. "It's parade time!" he cried.

The birds sang, the band played, and the people of Arendelle cheered as the parade wound its way through town. Anna was so happy she couldn't stop smiling.

The spring parade was perfect!

Later Anna and Elsa celebrated the successful parade. "We did it, Anna!" Elsa said. "The parade was just like when we were kids!"

"No," Anna said, grinning at her sister. "It was even better."

Disney

Bambi

The Spring Adventure

Early one morning, Thumper hopped through a thicket to visit his friend Bambi.

"Wake up," the bunny whispered to the sleeping fawn. "Let's go on a special spring adventure!"

Bambi stirred and gave a great big yawn. "I have to tell my mother where we're going."

"You can't do that," Thumper said. "It's a secret. Besides, she'd never let us go."

With that, the friends hopped away through the woods.

A few minutes later, Bambi and Thumper spotted their skunk friend. “Good morning, Flower,” Thumper said.

“Thumper wants to go on a special spring adventure,” Bambi said. “Do you want to come along?”

“Oh, gosh! I do,” Flower said. “But would you tell me what we’re doing?”

Thumper puffed up his chest and said, “I want to show you what the beavers build on water!”

Bambi and Flower looked at each other. It sure sounded exciting!

The three friends didn't notice a red bird perched on a branch above them.

The bird, named Red, was a friend of Bambi's mother. He flew to her and told her where the young prince was headed.

"Maybe it would be good for Bambi and his friends to explore on their own," Bambi's mother said. "Would you mind keeping an eye on them?"

Red agreed.

Meanwhile, Thumper and Flower were hard at work trying to push Bambi through a tight thicket.

"Why are we going this way?" Bambi asked.

"We can't go the regular way," Thumper whispered. "We are really close to the meadow where all the bunnies graze—including my mama. If she sees us, she'll say I have to look after my silly sisters!"

Suddenly, some branches gave way and the three friends fell out onto the meadow.

Thumper's sisters saw them. They wanted to know what their big brother was up to, so they followed him. So did Red.

The three friends continued walking through the woods. Soon they came to a stream.

A beaver with big teeth and a large, flat tail walked up to them. "Who are you?" Bambi asked.

"My name is Slap," the beaver said. "Where are you going?"

Thumper hopped forward. "I wanted to show my friends what the beavers build on the river," he explained.

"We call it a dam," said Slap, "and I can show you the way."

A little while later, they arrived at the dam.

"Here we are," Slap said. Everywhere along the river, the beavers were busy. Some were in the water pushing logs while others were chopping down trees with their strong teeth.

"Come out onto the dam," Slap offered.

Thumper and Flower went first, and Bambi followed, a bit unstable on his legs. Soon they were balancing on the logs among the working beavers.

"Hey, this is fun!" Thumper shouted.

The dam started to shake.

"Help! Help, Thumper!" four little voices suddenly cried.

It was Thumper's younger sisters! They had gone out on the dam as it started to shake. Now the log they were sitting on was floating away!

"We have to rescue them!" Thumper exclaimed.

"Hurry—they are headed toward the waterfall!" Slap shouted.

Thumper's sisters were getting close to the waterfall!

A few minutes later, Slap and two other beavers reached the runaway log. They slapped their tails with all their might, and slowly but surely, they got the log to the riverbank.

Bambi stood in the water with Thumper perched on his head. One by one, Thumper pulled his sisters to safety.

"Oh, I'm so glad you are safe!" cried Bambi's mother as she led them into the meadow, where there was more sunlight. "Red was keeping an eye on you. He told us what happened."

Until then the friends had not noticed the bird who was flitting in the air above them.

Bambi's mother tapped her foot angrily. "You all must promise never to go off without telling someone first!" she said.

Once everyone was back on land, Thumper thanked the beavers for their bravery.

"You're welcome," said Slap. "Can you find your way home from here?"

"Nothing to it," Thumper said. "We live just around the thicket, and to the right."

Thumper began to lead the others through the woods. But he couldn't seem to find the path home, so they kept walking and walking. Soon the trees blocked the light from the fading sun, and the branches swayed, casting scary shadows all around.

"Uh, Thumper," Bambi said, "I think we might be lost."

"Oh, don't be silly," Thumper said. "There's nothing to be afraid of here—especially when you're with the bravest rabbit in the forest!"

Suddenly, Thumper hopped into something. "Aaaahhh!" he screamed.

Fortunately, it was not a monster that Thumper had run into. It was Bambi's mother!

"Oh, I'm so glad you are safe!" cried Bambi's mother as she led them into the meadow, where there was more sunlight. "Red was keeping an eye on you. He told us what happened."

Until then the friends had not noticed the bird who was flitting in the air above them.

Bambi's mother tapped her foot angrily. "You all must promise never to go off without telling someone first!" she said.

They all agreed, though Thumper didn't seem too happy about it.

"Good," said Bambi's mother. "Now let's go home. The sun has started to set."

Soon the group returned home.

"Good night, everyone," Flower said.

"Good night, Flower!" the others called.

Bambi then turned to Thumper and whispered, "Thanks for taking me on your special spring adventure."

Thumper smiled. He and his family went to their burrow. Soon the bunny was fast asleep, dreaming of his next adventure.

The Search for Five Easter Eggs

Minnie woke up extra early on a sunny Easter morning. She just loved Easter, especially because she and her friends always had a picnic.

She ran over to Mickey's house to meet up with the gang. Mickey was decorating the living room, and Goofy was trying to convince Donald to put on bunny ears. Daisy was painting five Easter eggs, one for herself and each of her friends.

"Come on, everyone, it's time to go outside and have our Easter picnic!" Minnie cheered.

As the group gathered their picnic supplies, Daisy put the basket of Easter eggs on the porch so she wouldn't forget it.

But just then, Pete walked by looking for trouble.

Hmmm, this looks like it could be fun, he thought, grabbing the basket.

“Hey, Mickey, happy eggless Easter!” Pete called out as he hopped away.

Mickey and the gang rushed to the window, but it was too late. Pete was already gone!

“Oh, no!” Minnie cried, running outside. “Pete took our eggs!”

The rest of the gang rushed out after her.

“Easter is ruined!” Donald said.

“Come on, gang, it’ll be okay,” Mickey said, trying to encourage his friends. “I’m sure there’s something else we can do. . . .” His voice trailed off as something caught his eye.

"Oh, boy!" Mickey said suddenly. He walked to a nearby tree and reached up to a low branch. His friends watched in shock as he pulled down one of the Easter eggs.

"You guys, we're going on a good old-fashioned Easter egg hunt!" Mickey exclaimed.

Everybody split up to cover more ground, but Donald was still discouraged. He was worried they would never find all five eggs in time for their picnic, and then their food would get cold.

As he was beginning to lose hope, Donald spotted something blue and pink beneath a bright green bush.

Hmmm, what could this be? Donald thought as he pushed the leaves aside.

“Hey, Goofy, I found one!” Donald shouted.

Goofy ran over to admire the egg Donald had found.

"Well, that's two already," Goofy said. "At this rate, we should have them all in no time—"

"And then we'll get to eat our delicious picnic!" Donald said, finishing Goofy's sentence.

As Goofy searched near the same bushes for more eggs, he heard Pluto bark. He ran over to find Pluto in a meadow, staring at a pile of sticks.

"Hmmm, well that's odd. Why are these sticks stacked like this?" Goofy asked Pluto.

Pluto barked again and then started picking up sticks with his mouth, hoping Goofy would help.

Goofy quickly caught on and began picking up sticks, too. They soon discovered that Pluto had found not just one but *two* eggs!

"Golly, get over here, guys!" Goofy shouted.

Mickey and Daisy ran into the meadow and cheered with Goofy and Pluto.

"Only one more egg!" Mickey announced.

Minnie and Daisy knew the last egg would be especially well hidden.

They headed toward the stream, the only place they hadn't checked yet.

While Minnie lifted branches and looked under bushes, something caught Daisy's eye. She had found the final egg! But there was a problem: it was *in* the water!

Minnie knew they didn't have long before the egg floated away, so she took off her shoes and jumped into the stream. Wading through the current, she caught the egg before it was swept out of reach.

"Woo-hoo!" Daisy cheered from the shore.

The cheering continued as Minnie appeared with the basket full of all five eggs. Daisy followed close behind with the basket containing their picnic.

Easter was saved!

"Happy Easter, everyone!" Mickey said. "Even you, Pete. Your little trick ended up making this Easter even more special!"

"Oh, great. That's exactly what I wanted," Pete responded with a huff.

But Pete couldn't stay upset for too long. The gang shared their picnic with him, and the food was still warm and delicious.

Disney·PIXAR

MONSTERS, INC.

Basket of Trouble

Inside Monsters, Inc., Sulley was coming out of a door on Scare Floor F, finishing his shift. As he and Mike headed for the locker room, they saw Charlie Proctor and George Sanderson standing outside another door.

"Hi, guys," George said. "I just scared an entire slumber party full of little kids. They were dressed up like bunnies . . . which was odd. But now I'm thinking I'll be the seventh best Scarer in no time!"

Charlie ran off to get started on his paperwork for Roz. As George turned to follow him, something made Sulley and Mike stop in their tracks and gasp. They both pointed at George's tail. Hanging off it was something terrible. Something awful! Something . . . human!

Spinning around at the sound of their gasps, George tried to see what had scared his friends. He spun until the object flew across the hall—right into Sulley's hands.

Sulley's eyes grew wide as he looked at the object. It was shaped almost like the bottom half of an egg, without the top. Then he realized exactly what it was: a basket. A *human's* basket. Sulley let out a very un-monstrous squeak and threw it at Mike.

Back and forth the basket flew among them: to Sulley, to George, to Mike, and then back to George.

None of them wanted to touch it!

"This is—" screeched George.

"The worst!" yelled Sulley.

"Keep it away from me!" shouted Mike.

Finally, Mike shouted, "Guys, keep it together! This is a human object, remember? We can't just stand here in the hallway with it!"

George nodded. "You're right," he said. "If Charlie sees me with this, I'll get another 2319. And I can't have another run-in with the CDA." He reached behind him and patted his backside. "My fur just grew back."

Mike took a deep breath. "Okay, first things first. We need to get it to the locker room and stay there until we figure out a real plan."

"How are we going to get it there?" asked Sulley. "I don't want to touch it again."

Mike grabbed his gym bag and pulled out a pair of shoes, a hammer, and a pair of sunglasses. "No, no, no," he whispered to himself. Finally, he found his oven mitts. "Here you go, big guy!"

Sulley put them on and carefully picked up the basket.

The three monsters made their way down the hall. Bursting into the locker room, they ran right into Charlie.

“Charlie,” George said, “what are you doing here?”

“Why wouldn’t I be here?” Charlie asked, confused.

Mike didn't hesitate. "Because, Charlie," he said, "we thought you were with Roz for the big award."

"Big award?" Charlie repeated.

Mike nodded. "I heard the CDA wanted to see you . . . something about a special badge for your help with those 2319s. You really should get going!"

Full of excitement, Charlie raced out the door.

The trio of monsters sighed in relief. They needed to get the basket back through its proper door—fast!

But just then, the locker room door swung open and a group of monsters walked in.

“Hey, fellas,” one of the monsters said, greeting them. “Just grabbing my odorant.” Noticing the basket in Sulley’s hand, the monster looked curious. “What’s that? Did management send us new scaring gear? ’Cause that thing is frightening! Look at all that pink. Let me take a look.”

“No!” Sulley shouted, moving the basket away. “I mean, nah, don’t bother. It’s just a prototype. Didn’t even work.”

Acting fast, George jumped onto a bench. All eyes turned to him. "Um, hey, so . . . have you heard the one about the . . . oven mitts?"

The group of monsters waited for George to go on.

"They were so hot they were cool," he finally finished.

As the other monsters groaned, Sulley slipped out. Mike hesitated. "George, tell 'em the one about where cows go for some fun," he said.

Before George could say anything, another monster jumped in. "The *moo*-vies," he answered. "We've heard that one. But have you heard *this* one?"

As the monster told his joke, Mike followed Sulley to the Scare Floor and called back the doors George had gone through that day.

Sulley popped his head through each doorway, but he had no idea what he was looking for.

Then Sulley remembered that George had mentioned bunnies! He and Mike opened one door after another. They didn't find any long-eared, fluffy-tailed critters, but Sulley did run into a very affectionate cow.

Then Mike saw something green sticking out from under one of the doors. It was a piece of grass—the same grass that was in the basket!

When they opened the door, they found the slumber party full of kids wearing bunny ears. Sulley tiptoed into the room. All he had to do was put the basket down and get out of there before anyone noticed him.

"Easter Bunny? Is that you?"

Sulley froze.

One little girl was wide-awake, staring at him with big tear-filled eyes. Then Sulley noticed that she didn't have a basket next to her like the other girls.

"Easter Bunny?" the little girl said again.

Not sure what else to do, Sulley put the oven mitts on his horns, then began to hop like the bunny he saw on the television in the room.

"Did you bring back my basket?" the girl asked.

Sulley held out the basket. The girl bounded to her feet and grabbed the handle.

Sulley had begun to walk back toward the door when . . .

"Easter Bunny," the girl said again, stopping him, "you're blue. And you don't really look like a bunny."

"I'm in disguise," he whispered, turning for the door again.

As Sulley opened the door back to Monsters, Inc., he heard the little girl whisper, “Silly blue bunny.” Sulley smiled and hopped through the door.

Once he was safely back on Scare Floor F, he and Mike both let out relieved breaths. That had been too close.

"Those were some interesting moves back there," said Mike. "If scaring doesn't work out, maybe you can get a job being an Easter bunny—whatever that is."

Sulley shrugged. "A Scarer's gotta do what a Scarer's gotta do," he replied as George caught up to them.

"Hey, George," Mike said, "you should see Sulley's new trick. Show 'im, Sulley. Hop to it!"

The big blue monster smiled and began to hop down the hall. Behind him, George and Mike just laughed.

The Great Egg Hunt

To celebrate the end of a rainy week and the first day of spring, Pongo and Perdita had a surprise in store!

"We're going to have an egg hunt!" Perdita said.

"We have the eggs here," Pongo said. "We need everyone to help with painting and hiding. Are you all up for it?"

The puppies barked happily.

Soon every puppy had an egg, and they were all having tremendous—and rather messy—fun making their eggs unique. Patch and Lucky couldn't stop laughing as they got messier . . . and messier . . . and messier.

When their eggs were completely painted and dry, Patch and Lucky split up to hide them. The other puppies did the same.

Lucky wandered down to a fence near the barn. He found a small knothole in one of the fence posts that was just the right size for an egg. He placed it in the hole and nudged it inside.

Lucky was sure his brother would never find this hiding spot!

Meanwhile, Patch had headed straight to the woods that bordered the farm.

There was a tree with large and twisty roots that Patch thought could hide his egg. He found a small hollow and placed the egg under it.

Tail wagging, he ran back toward the farm.

Patch and Lucky joined a crowd of other puppies who were trotting back toward the barn proudly, each certain they'd found the best hiding spot of all.

Pongo counted them as they arrived, and once every puppy was present, he barked for their attention. "Is everyone ready for the egg hunt?" he called, and the puppies cheered.

“Ready, set . . . go!” Perdita called, and the puppies scattered happily across the farm and woodlands.

“Why don’t we look together?” Lucky suggested to Patch. “I want to see if you can find my hiding spot!”

“Me too—that sounds like fun!” Patch said before hurrying off toward the fence where he’d seen Lucky go earlier.

Pongo and Perdita watched the puppies search until they turned to see one of the farm hens staring into the empty egg box and clucking in distress.

"Oh, Perdita!" Henrietta cried. "My egg is missing! I laid one of my eggs in this box and now it's gone!"

Pongo and Perdita looked at each other in dismay. Henrietta's egg had surely been mixed up with the eggs for the hunt!

Meanwhile, it hadn't taken Patch long to find Lucky's hiding spot. Lucky had accidentally left paw tracks in the mud!

"Better luck next time," Patch teased. "Now it's your turn!"

Lucky sniffed and walked toward the woods, nose to the ground.

It took Lucky longer to find Patch's hiding spot.

When they arrived at the tree, Lucky sniffed around as he hunted for the egg. Patch watched in satisfaction, pleased with his clever hiding spot.

Then Lucky suddenly gave a disappointed cry. "Oh, no! It's broken!"

"What? How?" said Patch.

His brother had found the right hiding place, but he'd also found colorful broken eggshells.

Then they noticed tiny footprints leading away from the hiding spot.

"It must have hatched!" Patch said in surprise. "Look!"

"Now what do we do?" Lucky asked.

"We should find it as quick as we can, before it gets hurt!" Patch said.

The brothers put their noses to the ground and began to sniff, soon picking up the scent of the baby chick. It had gone up the hill toward the cow pasture.

Lucky ran forward, barking, and the cow looked up in surprise, backing away from the baby chick.

Unfortunately, the chick ran away from the cow . . . and away from Lucky.

It was heading for the barn!

Patch and Lucky ran into the barn after it, but it was too dark to see the chick anywhere. Then Patch heard a quiet peeping and looked up.

The chick was on top of a stack of hay bales, and the stack was swaying dangerously.

The pups braced their paws against the stack, trying to steady it.

The top hay bale suddenly fell toward the ground, taking the chick with it. To the puppies' relief, the chick landed safely on the soft hay.

But the chick was on the move again!

"Patch! That way!" Lucky said, and the two ran out the barn door.

Patch and Lucky couldn't tell where the chick had gone.

At last, Lucky leaned against the wall of a doghouse. "This is impossible, Patch!"

But then they heard a familiar sound.

Sitting in the doghouse, curled up on a blanket, was the baby chick! It was peeping softly in its sleep.

"Mom, Dad! I found where Patch hid his egg . . ." Lucky said.

"But it was actually a chick!" Patch explained.

Henrietta overheard and clucked in delight. "My little chick! You found it! Thank you so much!"

"Oh, how wonderful!" Perdita said. "But now you don't have an egg, Lucky. . . ."

"That's okay," said Lucky. "I think Patch and I have had enough hunting for one day!"